POTSY
(And Lucky)

by
COLENE COPELAND

cover
Hannele Gauthier

Jordan Valley Heritage House

POTSY

Copyright 1997, by Colene Copeland

Jordan Valley Heritage House
43592 Hwy. 226
Stayton, Oregon 97383

Manufactured in the U.S.A.

Library of Congress
97-073116

ISBN: 0-939810-19-0 (Hardcover)
ISBN: 0-939810-20-4 (Paperback)

First Edition

POTSY
(Priscilla Series Book #6)

Dedication
To the next generation in my family:
Jessica, Jason
& Elisa

To Quinlan & Connor,

Pig Out On Books!

Colleen Copeland
2007

Contents

Chapter 1.

Look at Me, Somebody!

Potsy watched with a sad and lonely face as another family walked right by the farm hogs heading straight for the Pot Bellied Pigs in the center of the long farrowing* barn. She and her family were snubbed again. Poor things.

The pig spoke greetings, smiled, shouted and jumped up and down, trying to stop families. But nothing worked. They kept walking, even when she said, "Please stop," to their backs.

Potsy was a lovely, rusty red farm hog with a white band around her middle. In the center of her forehead, looking forever like an artist had brushed it there, was a dab of white.

She was three weeks old. Like all pigs her

----
*(fair-o-ing)

1

age, she could walk and talk as well as her mother, Little Prissy. Maybe walk even better, after all, Little Prissy was getting on in years.

Folks who were interested in a pig for a pet came on Tuesdays and Thursdays each week to look at the Pot Bellies.

It must be nice, Potsy thought as she nibbled away at her breakfast, to have people admire you, to pet you and say how cute you are. Nobody ever asks for one of us to be a pet. Potsy wondered if she and the other farm hogs were inferior in some way.

Her thoughts were interrupted by Arthur, one of her six younger brothers.

"You eat too much," Arthur said slowly in a caring way. No one knew exactly why, but Arthur always talked, in a slow, pleasant way like someone from the south.

Potsy leveled a disapproving glance toward her brother.

"Mind your own business, pig."

"Well, ya do eat too much, Potsy," Arthur pointed out. "You're gonna get sick."

Potsy knew she ate too much. She didn't mind her brother knowing. Being reminded of it is what she didn't like.

"I don't want you to get sick. You are my favorite sister," Arthur continued, trying to be nice.

"Arthur, you are a such a pushover. Yesterday, I heard you tell Nel that she was your favorite sister," Potsy informed him. "She told everybody."

"Oh!" Arthur hung his little head. But he was a bright little pig and thought fast. "Well, yesterday Nel *was* my favorite sister, but today, you are." How clever he was.

Potsy laughed. She loved her brother.

"But you really do eat too much," Arthur said again very slowly as he backed up toward his mother and nestled in with the rest of the family sleeping there on the wooden floor of their pen.

An Oregon Bluejay hopped through the front door. Jays are loud. This one squawked, disturbing Potsy's thoughts.

Her thoughts, as usual, were on the Pot Bellies. Since she first learned about them, she had been curious. Potsy had asked her mother lots of questions. Some questions got no answer. Many times Little Prissy put her off by saying, "I don't really know Potsy. I'll ask Mama." By Mama, she meant, of course, the farmer's wife, who talks with Prissy regularly in a most bizarre' but understanding way.

What Potsy really wanted more than

anything, was to go down to that part of the old farrowing barn where the Pot Bellies lived, and have a look.

Sometimes Papa, their owner, turned her family loose to run up and down the hallway while he cleaned their pen. Potsy figured the sooner the pen was dirty the sooner she would be turned out. So naturally, she was messing up the pen. She overturned the empty water pan with her nose and pushed it across the floor. It squeaked. But it served the purpose, which was to push all the cedar shavings on the floor over by the wall. Since Papa likes to see the entire floor spread evenly, for their comfort and cleanliness, he was sure to notice the bare floor and want to clean it up.

As Potsy kept on messing up the pen the hot, fall evening began to cool down. A dark cloud drifted in over the farm. The wind picked up, followed by thunder and lightning. The storm grew loud and shook the old barn.

No one slept or even rested any longer, for the noise. For Little Prissy's pigs, this was their first storm. The big window in the back of the pen, rattled loudly. The frightened babies moved nervously about the pen, crowding close to their mother.

Little Prissy was reminded of the great

storm the night when she and Tom Cat had to go down to the farmhouse in the pouring rain for help. Frightened by the storm, the neighbor's fun-loving burro, Piston, had come in to the farrowing barn through the big front door kicking and braying. He caused death and destruction that night, but he didn't mean to do it. After a while everyone forgave him, and he was invited to make his home here on the farm.

"So many memories," Prissy thought.

As the storm passed, a gentle rain cooled the evening. The pitter-patter on the roof calmed the worry brought on by the thunder and lightning. Before long, the pigs were again sleeping soundly and enjoying the change in temperature.

Being Sunday, Papa and Mama had fed the hogs early. It would be morning before they returned to the barn. Potsy hoped she could mess up the pen faster than her mother could clean it up.

How Potsy longed to be noticed, to be somebody special like she believed the Pot Bellies must surely be. She wished she could just see them. But after all, she was a mere farm hog, and maybe no one would ever pay any attention to her.

She'd have to wait and see.

Chapter 2.

The Visit

The next morning was glorious. The clouds and rain had given way to a clear blue sky. Golden sun rays poked through the wide front door. A country fresh fragrance permeated round about. High in the apple trees song birds welcomed the morning. Robins flicked merrily on the damp ground, plucking out unsuspecting worms for breakfast.

Papa made his first appearance of the morning. In one hand he carried a three and a half gallon milk bucket by its bale, in the other a scrawny yellow cat was pressed to his chest. Cats were often thrown out of cars in front of the farm. Such a cruel way to dispose of unwanted animals.

"What's in the bucket?" Arthur asked Papa as he came near their pen. Papa did not

6

understand the pig's question.

"Well, hello little fellow. Are you enjoying the sunshine?" Papa smiled at Arthur and his family. Papa always asked friendly questions. The pigs seemed to understand him, but he did not understand the language of the pigs.

Arthur soon learned that Papa's bucket was full of zucchini, fresh from the garden and gigantic in size. Papa said good morning to all the hogs as he cut the zucchini in large chunks and passed them around. At the sound of Papa's voice the hogs sprang to their feet, snorting and grunting happily. Breakfast was being served. Papa saw to it that each of them got all they wanted. The zucchini was a special treat.

When he served the morning pellets in Prissy's pen he took a long hard look at the bare floor just like Potsy knew he would. Prissy had tried to spread the cedar shavings around some, but as soon as her back was turned Potsy messed them up again. The pig was determined to be turned out.

"I've never seen such a bare bone floor, Prissy. After a bit I'll take care of it for you," Papa said.

The plan was working. Potsy smiled a triumphant smile.

Mama came in from the orchard with her

apron full of apples.

"You're gonna spoil these hogs," Papa grinned.

"Look who's talking. I saw you carry in a bucket full of something from the garden," she laughed.

Mama headed straight for Little Prissy's pen. She always heads straight for Little Prissy's pen because Prissy is her favorite. The little sow was on her feet munching on her morning ration of pellets Papa had put in her feed pan. All the young pigs were in their corner creep enjoying their portion of starter pellets.

Prissy's mouth was too busy to talk, so Mama made a tour around the barn. She visited and checked on all the pigs. There was one new, rescued Pot Belly. Some ladies had chased this one down in a Christmas tree farm. It was not easy. The pig was afraid and would not come to them. Food was left there for two days in a row in the same place. The third day, the pig was standing there waiting for more. With a full belly the pig began to trust the ladies and allowed them to pick him up. And as usual, Papa and Mama ended up with the pig. Mama named him "Lucky".

"He's looking a little better today, don't you think so?" Papa asked when he saw Mama was having a look at Lucky.

The pig was still a little stand-offish. As he ate his food he kept looking around as if expecting trouble.

"Poor thing is so thin. But, today he's not snapping at his food. I guess his belly is getting full, and he's a lot more friendly," Mama replied. "I wonder how long he went without food? There wasn't much grass to eat around those Christmas trees."

"The little grass that was available to him was so full of bug spray, he's probably sick from it," Papa added. "Let's give him a good bath tonight and take him to the vet in the morning."

"Yes, let's do that," Mama agreed.

Papa headed back to the front of the barn to clean Little Prissy's pen. Potsy will be happy about that.

Already, he had closed the back barn door so Prissy's family could not escape. He would close the front door for the same reason. Papa said he was getting too old to chase hogs.

Good fortune had smiled on Potsy. As soon as her gate was open she ran down the hallway as fast as her little legs could carry her.

The farrowing barn had a long hallway down the center. It divided two rows of 10'x10' pens. A distance of about 50 feet lay between her pen and the little apartment pen where the first Pot Belly lived.

Potsy spotted Mama standing by the new pig's place. How nice. Mama's presence gave her the courage to proceed. After all Potsy was just a little pig. This was her first visit away from home and she was kind of scared. Potsy knew she was somehow different from the Pot Bellies. They might not like her.

"My goodness Potsy," Mama exclaimed. "You sure are a fast runner."

The little pig loved the compliment. It was the first one she had ever been given. In fact, she liked it so much she hoped it would not be the last.

Lucky took one look at Potsy and ran out the back door of his apartment to the outside yard, out of sight. He was midnight black, all over.

"Scrud," Potsy said to herself. "Now, what do I do."

Mama called and called to Lucky, but he would not budge. Potsy's time was limited. Papa would be calling her back soon. He was a fast pen cleaner.

Potsy thought of hiding. Maybe one pig would not be missed. Quickly, her eyes examined the hallway for a place to hide. There was not one good place.

Mama felt sorry for Potsy. She felt sure the pig had made a special effort to see Lucky, and now, Lucky was not cooperating.

Potsy was desperate. Using her best manners, she pleaded with Lucky.

"Please come in. I've come to visit. I won't be allowed to stay out very long."

Being ever so cautious, Lucky poked his head inside the back door of his place. Seeing no danger and remembering a little food was left in his feeding pan, he ventured back in. But by this time Papa was calling for Little Prissy and her babies to come on back.

Fortunately for Potsy, Little Prissy was also visiting with her grown daughters who have pigs of their own. So she did not return immediately when Papa called.

Papa didn't mind. He let the mother visit with her daughters and went about rounding up the pigs.

Mama motioned to Papa to let him know that Potsy needed a minute. Again, the pig was pleased by Mama's kindness to her.

"I'll be back to get you in a few minutes, Potsy," Mama said. "Right now Papa needs help in rounding up your brothers and sisters." She headed back up the hallway, herding pigs, who were running all over the place enjoying their freedom.

As soon as Mama was out of hearing range, a Pot Bellied sow in the apartment across the hall from Lucky suddenly became loud and mean. It was scary for such a little pig.

"Git out of here pig, go back up where you belong. We don't need anyone like you down here poking your nose in," the sow croaked.

The sow had taken Potsy quite by surprise. Frightened, she turned around to see the hateful eyes of a white, full grown Pot Belly scowling angrily at her.

"I just came down to visit Lucky," Potsy said slowly, using all the courage she could muster up.

"You came down here to snoop and cause trouble! Admit it!" the sow shouted.

"No I didn't," Potsy blubbered, almost in tears. Never had she heard such cruel, unkind words.

Lucky became angry at what he was hearing from the sow.

"Leave that little pig alone you ugly old sow," he shouted.

Potsy was surprised and puzzled. Surprised by the sow's bad temper and puzzled that Lucky had taken up for her instead of siding with a Pot Belly like himself.

The sow's cruelty had hurt the kind little pig and she felt it all the way to the bone. Never having heard such anger and bad temper before, she gave up. Completely beaten, Potsy turned slowly and trotted back up the hall toward her pen.

Lucky called after her.

"Please come back again, little pig. I want you to come back."

The way Potsy was feeling, she would never have the nerve to go back down to see Lucky ever again.

Chapter 3.

Potsy Is Warned

After hearing about Potsy's painful experience, Little Prissy tried her best to console her dejected daughter. But Potsy would not be consoled. She was miserable.

"I just wanted to have a look at the Pot Bellies," Potsy told her mother. "Lucky was nice. But that old white sow was mean to me. She said unkind words. The kind you wouldn't allow us to say. You wouldn't like her, Mother."

"Better stay at home and not go down there," one of Potsy's sisters cautioned.

For now, at least, Potsy intended taking her advice. But she knew she must try again. She must find a way to thank Lucky who had shown her kindness. And there was more. Potsy had not yet satisfied her curiosity. She had not learned what it was about the Pot Bellies that made

14

people want one for a pet.

"When I was a little pig and my mother wanted to send a message to someone, or find out something, she sent Tom Cat," Prissy told Potsy. "She and Tom Cat were great friends. Unlike us, the cats are free to go anywhere they want, and, this particular cat was very clever. He remained my friend too, long after my mother died. Then one day he died of old age," Prissy looked sad as she recalled the death of her mother and Tom Cat.

"Perhaps I can make friends with one of the barn cats. Perhaps I can have a messenger too," Potsy said.

"Perhaps you can, Potsy. Perhaps you can," was her mother's sleepy reply.

With a renewed spark of hope Potsy was able to fall asleep.

Little Arthur rooted in next to his sister for the night. There was really no doubt about it. Arthur truly did love Potsy best.

When morning arrived, so did Mama. She opened their gate, sat down on the straw bedding and began to pet each of the pigs.

Potsy wondered about a couple of things. Did the Pot Bellies understand Mama the way her mother does? And, how about Mama for a messenger? A good idea, but was it proper to ask her? She wasn't sure. Little Prissy had taught her babies manners, just as her mother had taught them to her.

"Your family is gorgeous, Prissy," Mama said, reaching to give yet another pig a belly rub.

"That one is curious about the Pot Bellies," Prissy told Mama.

"Curious? Oh yes, she was the one trying to visit Lucky. But I don't think she saw much of him. He ran and hid in his back yard. The little stinker. He is about two years old, I think, and black. He is as black as the LaBrea tar pits. Small and cute, that's Lucky. When we get him caught up on all the meals he's missed, he'll be cuter." Mama smiled.

Little Prissy did not tell Mama about the sow's cruel words to her daughter. Potsy wondered why.

Potsy was listening to their conversation. She understood some of what Mama said and hoped if there was more said about Lucky, she would understand.

Today Potsy planned to watch out for barn cats and look them over. Lately, only a couple of cats ever came near their pen. Little Prissy talked to them sometimes. Potsy knew the one she chose must be smart and trustworthy.

When it's cold outside the cats curl up

with the pigs under the heat lamps. In that respect, they are smart. The few that came by were friendly enough, but Potsy thought them to be totally selfish and independent. Maybe she had been wrong, hopefully she had.

Papa named the stray cat "Chance". He looks much better than he did when he first arrived. Papa had worked him over real good. He had brushed off the mud, picked out the burrs and put salve and butterfly bandaids on his cuts.

Arthur didn't know it when he made friends with Chance, but he was doing Potsy a big favor.

"Where did you come from cat?" Arthur asked slowly as the big yellow creature trotted through the front door behind Papa.

"Can't recall," the cat answered through a smirky smile.

"What do you mean you can't recall?" Arthur asked.

"Don't be so nosey, son," Little Prissy reminded Arthur. "If Chance doesn't want to tell you where he came from he doesn't have to," Prissy was being polite to the newcomer.

Chance gave the sow a friendly glance and replied.

"My problem is, I really can't recall. My

owner put me in a cage in the back of his truck to take me to the Humane Society. I had belonged to his wife. Problem was, she went away and did not come back. Can't say that I blamed her. He got mad and shoved me into that cage and said, 'You are going to the Humane Society, Cat. I'll show her.' Well I've heard what happens to unwanted cats at the Humane Society, so on the way to town I managed to get the door to the cage open and jumped out of the truck. When I jumped, I went flying into the car behind us. Ker-whap! The next thing I knew I woke up in the roadside ditch with a headache. I only remembered that part this morning. But I still don't remember where home was. And that's the truth."

"I believe you Chance," Potsy said sweetly.

"Me too," Arthur added.

A couple of Potsy's brothers thought the cat was just making up a story, but their mother told them to keep quiet.

A visiting family came in with Mama to see the Pot Bellies. The man was large and in a business suit. The woman with him was smoking a cigarette. Papa will make her put it out. One spark in the dry wheat straw could set it on fire. Not to mention that the smoke stinks.

With their parents were twin boys about 9 or 10 years of age. Like everyone else, they hurried on back to the Pot Bellies. The boys glanced at the farm hogs but kept on walking. One held his nose, an unnecessary thing to do. This hog barn never smelled bad. It smelled of wheat straw and cedar shavings, clean and fresh.

Visitors passing them by were of no concern to any of them, except Potsy. She wondered why her mother and the other farm hogs weren't bothered by being passed up. She wondered why it bothered only her. Was she different?

In the midst of wondering, Papa came in with another Pot Bellied pig to add to the collection. Abruptly, he turned on his heels and carried the pig into the office.

"Almost forgot," he was heard saying. "I know just the family for you." The pig was allowed to play around in the office while Papa telephoned a family on his list who wanted a pig like this one.

In the mean time, Little Prissy was watching Potsy. As she watched she finally realized what it was that Potsy longed for.

"My sweet little girl," Prissy said, concerned for the welfare of her daughter. "You had better let well enough alone. If it's attention you want, then you'd better be careful where that attention takes you. Are you jealous of the Pot Bellies because they get attention? If you are, listen to me. People come and get those pigs because they are smaller than we are. They take them out of here, to their homes, and make pets out of them. Is that what you want? To be taken out of here? *Those* pigs are here because *people* have mistreated them. We are lucky Potsy. We have the very best of everything. Think what you are doing, or the next thing you know you will be carried out of here under some *person's* arm and I will never see you again."

Potsy stared at her mother with large inquiring eyes. She had no desire to be taken away from the farm or her mother. She was merely curious about the Pot Bellies. Was her mother right? Was she jealous? Would she be carried out under some stranger's arm, just for being curious? So much to consider for such a little pig.

Chapter 4.

The Farmhouse

Papa and Mama came by Prissy's pen and picked up Arthur without a word of explanation. This disturbed every farm hog who was near enough to see the pig being carried out the front door.

On their minds were two main questions. "What's going on here and where are they taking, Arthur?"

Potsy was really worried. Hadn't her mother talked to her about being taken away. And now, Arthur was being whisked off.

It was only Little Prissy who was not surprised.

"They have taken him to the veterinarian to be checked over. He'll be back before you know it."

"Why Mother? What's wrong with him?"

21

Potsy asked.

"Haven't you noticed? Arthur hasn't been eating. He says he isn't hungry. But a pig who is not hungry is not well. The rest of you are healthy and gaining weight. At first I thought he was eating a little less, and then I noticed he wasn't eating at all. I told Mama. She said when he was born his weight was normal. But now, he is thin, too thin. The doctor will know what to do. He will fix Arthur up in no time. I've seen it happen before." Little Prissy didn't fool anybody. She was plenty worried and they all knew it. But no one said so.

Potsy remembered when Arthur told her she ate too much. She felt a little ashamed that she had not paid more attention to Arthur's eating habits. If she had, maybe she could have helped him. She hoped with all her heart that Arthur would be all right.

It was nearly noon when her little brother was returned to the pen.

Mama reported to Prissy. "Well, he stumped the vet."

Arthur was trying to tell his brothers and sisters too. He and Mama were both talking at the same time. Arthur had gotten a vitamin shot. He hated it. But it was supposed to increase his appetite and help him to gain weight.

Arthur liked the ride in the truck. He rode in comfort in a large crate on lots of sweet smelling wheat straw. It was his first trip. Passing by other farms, he saw cattle and sheep grazing on pasture, but no hogs. He wondered why.

Arthur tried to explain the new music he had heard in the vet's office, but he did not know how. In the farrowing barn Papa kept the radio always tuned to KRKT, a local country station. Until today, all Arthur had ever heard was country music. What he heard he liked and he sure wished he knew how to explain it.

Mama was still there with something else on her mind.

"How would you like to go for a walk, Potsy?" Mama asked.

Potsy was so busy listening to her brother that when Mama reached down to pick her up she was totally unprepared. She let out a squeal loud enough to split the air. But Mama hung on to her.

"Sorry pig, didn't mean to scare you," Mama laughed, putting Potsy down in the hallway, outside the pen.

To calm her down, Papa threw a few food pellets in front of her. That always works. Mama let her nibble on them until they were all gone.

There was nothing wrong with Potsy's appetite. Hopefully she would follow them across the orchard to the farmhouse.

The pig was pleased and excited about being taken for an outing. Little Prissy knew it was just the thing this particular daughter needed.

"Come on Potsy," Papa coaxed. "Follow us, so we don't have to carry you. O.K.?"

Potsy did as she was asked, happy to have been invited. In fact, the little pig was having a great time.

Potsy's owners were totally surprised by her obedience. Usually the farm hogs are harder to move. They take off running. The Pot Bellies seldom do. For some reason the Pot Bellies will walk right along beside you and not run away. They may stray a short distance, but all you have to do is call them by name and they will return to you. Not so with the farm hogs. So, Potsy's unusual behavior brought her praises and compliments.

Papa was doing a lot of smiling. He knew what was going on. Every so often, Mama takes a pig to the house and tries to make a "Priscilla" out of it. But it never works. Priscilla was one in a million. She was pure pet and loved the house. But she too was a farm hog and all to soon, she outgrew the farmhouse.

Each time this happened, Papa went along with it, to make Mama happy. This time it was Potsy's turn.

Potsy loved the walk through the apple orchard. Fallen apples were hers for the taking, under each tree. There were a few rotted ones but not many. Papa and Mama pick them up as soon as they fall and feed them to the hogs. The fruit seldom has time to rot.

The little party walked slowly so the pig could enjoy her first time out of the barn.

When they reached the farmhouse Potsy followed them up the wide stairs and on to the back porch without incident. Once inside, the pig began to snoop. She ran from room to room checking things out. She preferred the rooms with carpeting. The tile and wood floors in the bath, kitchen and hallways were tricky. She slipped and slid on those.

It didn't take long to learn that going into the kitchen had its advantages. Food was being prepared in the kitchen, fresh fruits and vegetables from the garden. All she had to do was stand there and ask and each time she was rewarded with a bite or two of something.

Potsy's favorite item in the house was the refrigerator. When she heard the door to it being opened, she made a beeline for the kitchen, hoping for a handout. She made Mama and Papa laugh.

In a short period of time she learned many new things. The television was exciting. After Papa watched the news channel he switched to cartoons for Potsy.

"Your grandmother, Priscilla, loved to watch television, Potsy. Her favorite program was 'Hee Haw'. She loved Roy Clark's banjo music. She got really excited when she saw him put on his banjo. And, all the while he played the banjo, she danced."

"What she really did was stand there and shake her hiney," Mama laughed.

Papa took Potsy out to the backyard every little bit for a bathroom break. She was a fast learner.

Maggie, the old Springer Spaniel, also came in the house once in a while. Potsy had seen her in the barn. But Maggie preferred the out of doors and barked at the back door when she wanted out. Maggie and Potsy got along fine.

Potsy found plenty of soft pillows to nap on. In fact, everything about the house was nice and comfortable. But she never stopped thinking about her family in the farrowing barn or about Lucky.

Potsy began to worry when she was kept in the farmhouse over night. As much as she liked the comfort of the carpets and pillows, the television, the great food and all the attention, more than anything, she wanted her mother.

In the night, Potsy had been awakened by Maggie's barking. Maggie was outside. Papa got up to see what all the fuss was about. It was nothing unusual, just a few deer in the back yard. Often at night they come out of the timber in the back of the property. They feed on the fallen apples in the orchard and snoop around the yard.

Potsy had slept a restless sleep. She wondered if her family missed her as much as she missed them? When would she get to see them again?

Chapter 5.

Jealousy

Potsy refused to eat breakfast.

"She's not happy, Papa," Mama said. " I thought I could make a housepet out of her, but the situation is not the same. Priscilla's mother didn't want her. But this little thing has a family and a mother who will miss her baby." Mama reached down to pet Potsy on her back. "We will have to take her back to the barn after breakfast."

Papa nodded and smiled, knowing that Mama would have to come to that decision, sooner or later.

When Potsy heard she was going home, she changed her mind about breakfast. She ate everything in sight, some wheat toast, bites of egg, hash brown potatoes that were yummy, some warm milk and a handful of grapes.

28

It would be so fun to tell her family about the farmhouse. She could hardly wait. Before leaving for the barn, Mama thought of something she wanted to show Potsy.

"Potsy, let's go in to the bedroom for just a moment."

There was a large, beautifully framed picture of a pig on the wall. Mama pointed to it.

"Potsy, this is Priscilla, your grandmother. She lived in the house with us when she was little. She could turn the television on and off with her nose, answer the telephone and do lots of things that other pigs can't do. I guess because you look so much like her, I hoped you might want to take her place. But you have a family in the barn who want you. Priscilla didn't."

Potsy stared at the picture, having been told that she looked like Priscilla and wondered if that's what she really looked like. She also knew that Mama loved this pig a great deal. The little pig was glad she had been brought into the house. She had a feeling she was special to Mama and Papa. Maybe it was just because she looked like Priscilla. But no matter what, she was pleased that they had wanted her.

Upon reaching the farrowing barn Potsy was not immediately returned to her pen as she

expected to be. She stood in the hallway by
Mama and was bombarded with questions. The
farm hogs up front and her family were anxious
to know where she had been taken. The little
pigs looked out between the boards of the pen
and the sows stood with their front feet on the
tops of the boards. It was quite a moment for
Potsy. So much attention. Almost too much!

Arthur asked the most questions, in his
slow and caring manner. "Are you sick, Potsy?
Did they take you to the doctor too? Did you get
a shot in the butt? Did you hear the pretty
music?"

Potsy was saying "no" to all his questions.

"Are you back for good?" her mother
asked. "I hope you are."

In the midst of all the questions and
attention, Mama invited Potsy to come with her
down the hallway.

It looked like Potsy was going to get her
wish. The pig was in awe. Was she dreaming? It
must be true. They were headed toward Lucky's
place.

The barn doors had not been closed,
meaning only one thing. Potsy was being trusted
not to run away. She must never do anything to
violate that trust, she told herself. Potsy not only
looked like Priscilla, she was beginning to sound

like her as well.

With Mama along, Potsy was not so afraid. First off, she checked for the white sow. That pen was empty. That was wonderful.

Lucky was at home and another pig had been added to the pen.

"Hello pig. I hoped you'd come to visit me again." Lucky was glad to see Potsy.

When Mama opened the door to the pen Potsy noticed that the pen really looked more like a little house.

The Pot Bellies did not run out and Potsy did not run in. Actually, they stood there and stared at each other for a while, looking each other over.

Mama thought it was pretty funny. She and Potsy stepped inside the pen. Mama sat down in a chair. Potsy began to snoop. She asked herself a few questions. Why do the Pot Bellies get special treatment? Why was their floor carpeted? The place was painted a soft yellow and they even had a television set. How come?

Potsy was not aware that the pens are meant to be small apartments. They help prepare the Pot Bellies for the homes in which they will be living. Potsy was more than a little jealous, but she tried not to show it.

The little pig was greeted kindly by the

Pot Bellies.

"Hello! My name is Cooper, who are you?" the new pig asked.

"This is the farm hog I told you about. She visited me before you moved in," Lucky answered.

"I am Potsy. I am a farm pig and you are Pot Bellies," she said shyly.

The Pot Bellies laughed at Potsy in a very friendly way.

"You are sure right about our pot bellies," Lucky giggled. "Why don't farm hogs have pot bellies?"

"Don't ask me. I'm just a little pig." Now it was Potsy's turn to giggle. She was having a good time.

Mama listened and understood most of what the pigs were saying. No one knows why Mama can understand pigs. She just can. Perhaps its because she has been around them for a good many years, or better still, perhaps its because she truly cares about them and is interested in what they have to say.

Potsy nodded to the pen across the hall.

"Where is that mean old sow that was over there?"

"Don't worry about her. I think she's out in the pasture. I don't like that sow. She talked mean to you. I was afraid somebody would take me home for a pet before you'd get a chance to come and visit again," Lucky said sadly. "I like it here. I get plenty to eat, a good place to sleep and I am treated real well. That's more than I can say for the last place I lived."

"Was it bad?" Potsy asked.

"I lived on the hill behind the Christmas tree farm with the Cury family. They bought me for their spoiled kid named Chris. He lied to his parents when they asked if he had fed me. I got hungry, really hungry. Chris had a dog named Pepper. I talked the dog in to unlatching my gate so I could get out and try to find something to eat. There wasn't much grass to eat around the Christmas trees. But it kept me from starving. Muddy water was always available to drink if I looked hard enough. I was out there for several weeks before those nice ladies found me. They brought me food. Chris never did come to look for me."

Potsy listened to Lucky's sad story. Mama was watching the news on television.

"I'm glad you came here, Lucky. I wanted to come down here and thank you for being nice to me when that old sow was yelling at me," Potsy told him. "And please don't let them take you away. Maybe we can be friends. I don't have any friends yet. All I have is my mother and brothers and sisters. They are o.k., but a friend would be nice."

"How about me, too?" Cooper asked. "I'll be your friend after Lucky's gone."

Potsy looked at Mama. Could it be true? Was Lucky really leaving? Just when they were getting acquainted? Mama nodded.

Lucky is not the right name for this pig, Potsy told herself. Unlucky might fit him better. She did not want to think about it another minute.

"Sure Cooper, of course I want you for a friend. But don't make any plans. You'll be leaving too, just you wait and see."

She said good-bye to both her friends. Mama opened the gate and watched Potsy turn slowly and head back toward her mother.

Chapter 6.

Getting Attention

It was the only Saturday of the month when people are allowed to come to visit the Pot Bellies. Several families arrived early.

Arthur was eating better. Not as much as everybody else, but nevertheless, he was eating.

Potsy had heard just about all she could stand from the passerbyers on the subject of just "how wonderful and cute" the Pot Bellies were.

Potsy was using her mother's hind leg for a pillow. It just isn't fair, she told herself. Why do the Pot Bellies have all the comforts, when my only pillow is my mother's bony hind leg?

Little Prissy's family was still excited about Potsy's trip to the farmhouse. Over and over again, they asked their sister to tell about it, every little detail. So many questions for such a little pig. What did she eat there, and where

35

did she sleep? These were the questions of
interest. For these were the things they knew
about, eating and sleeping.

"Did Mama tell you why she took you to
the house?" her mother asked.

"Yes, Mother. You know how she liked
having your mother in the house and since I look
like her, she wanted me to take her place. I liked
the house but I didn't want to stay away from
you. It was nice and comfortable. The food was
great. You can't believe what all came out of the
refrigerator! Stuff that I had never seen before.
I didn't know what most of it was, but it was
good," Potsy told her.

"All food tastes good to you, Potsy,"
Arthur said slowly, teasing his sister.

Twice before noon, families left the barn
with their new pets, on a leash. Potsy watched
closely to see if this was Lucky's unlucky day. So
far it was not.

It was the middle of the afternoon when
Potsy woke up from one of her many naps and
looked into the eyes of a lovely young girl who
stood by the pen, staring down at her. She had
long, brown braids and kind, brown eyes to
match. She said nothing but stood there leaning
against the front boards of the pen, smiling.

Potsy wondered if the girl was real or if

she was left over from a dream. After a moment, the curious little pig got up and took a few steps toward her. Was she an angel?

"Hello little pig," the girl said softly. "Did anyone ever tell you how beautiful you are?"

Potsy looked up slowly. She looked behind her and to each side. She could not believe the girl was talking to her. Beautiful? She thinks I'm beautiful?

Prissy and her pigs came to their feet and stared at their visitor. They had an honest to goodness, real, live visitor. She asked if they would come closer so she could pet them.

"My name is Elsa. Do you all have names? I will ask your owner and then I can call each of you by your true name. Guess what? I am suppose to be back there with my family looking at the Pot Bellies. They want one for a pet. I prefer pigs like yourselves. Oh, I know you get too big and we can't keep you in the house, but I don't care, even if I'd have to keep you in a barn or a pasture, I prefer you guys. You have character."

Prissy's family was not used to being spoken to by outsiders. Frankly, that didn't bother them one iota, except of course, for Potsy. Potsy took an immediate liking to the girl. She loved the compliments and besides that, Elsa had answered a question for her. One she had given a lot of thought.

Farm hogs get too big to be house pets. That's the reason. That's why they get passed by. Potsy was learning, a little at a time.

But Elsa was not interested in a house pet. She preferred farm hogs because of their "character". Potsy was pleased knowing she had character, even though wasn't sure what it was. It sounded nice.

Elsa's father called to her, "Come on Elsa. We are trying to choose. Come and help us make the decision. Your sister likes a little, male named Lucky. See what you think."

"No, not Lucky," Potsy cried. "Please don't take Lucky." Elsa and her father did not understand Potsy.

Lucky did not cooperate with Elsa's family. He ran outside in his yard and hid. Elsa's mother liked Bonnie Lu, an older Pot Belly. Bonnie Lu was friendlier, much friendlier. She took food from their hands and laid down on their feet to be petted and get a belly rub. The children's father didn't really care which one they got. He liked them all. He just wanted the family to all be satified with their choice.

Papa and Mama never allow a pig to go home with anybody until the entire family has bonded with the pig. It looks like this family would have to come back another day.

Papa's biggest concern was for the pig. He felt responsible in getting the pig the best home possible. Lucky did not bond with this family. There had to be a reason. Bonnie Lu liked them well enough, but only the mother wanted her. The family definitely needed more time to choose.

Potsy laughed her head off when she heard that Lucky did not cooperate with this family. She was pleased as punch when Elsa bent over and kissed her on the head on her way out, and whispered in her ear.

"I know you are not looking to be adopted little pig. Too bad. You are cuter than all the Pot Bellies put together."

When Mama saw Elsa's interest in Prissy's family she was pleased. Mama preferred farm hogs over the Pot Bellies. Perhaps that why she hadn't taken a Pot Belly into the house.

If Mama had known at the time that Elsa wanted Potsy for her very own, perhaps she would have discouraged the girl and tried to funnel her interests in a different direction. As for now, she only suspected the girl's interests and hoped that she was wrong.

But on the other hand, she wanted Potsy

be happy.

"Aren't they a great looking litter of pigs?" Mama asked.

Elsa smiled broadly. "I just love them all. What are their names?"

Mama pointed them out in the order of their birth.

"Potsy has five older sisters, Alice, Nel, Sheila, Little Spoon and Sarah. Potsy is next. Then all the boys were born, Alvin, Pepper, Thomas, Carl, Cy and Arthur, the youngest. Little Spoon was named after a Native American boy who came to visit one day. He asked me to name a pig after his Indian name. So I did."

"I love Potsy. She is the most adorable animal I have ever seen. Look at the kindness of her eyes. I never knew a pig to have such eyes. Of course, I haven't seen very many, but I just love her. She is so sweet. May I come again and spend time with this family?"

Elsa made Mama a little uneasy, but at the same time she could not deny the child's wishes.

"Yes you may come and see them whenever you wish."

Prissy hoped that Potsy was finally satisfied. She had gotten all the attention she desired and more.

Even Arthur sort of liked the attention. But the poor little pig was too sick again to enjoy it. Rather than see his mother worry, he kept his problem all to himself. And that was the wrong thing to do.

Arthur had been to the doctor. But doctors can only do so much. The little pig's condition was much worse than anyone suspected.

Chapter 7.

A Sad Day

A family dropped by the farrowing barn on a day when visitors were not invited nor expected. Papa had a big sign out front that clearly stated, "Pot Bellied pig viewing on Tuesdays and Thursdays each week and the first Saturday of the month. Hours 10:00 to 4:00."

It was about 10:30 on Monday morning. This family was loud. When they came through the front door they could be heard all over the barn. There were two boys about 9 and 11 years old. One of them had a stick and commenced beating on the pens. The parents yelled obscene words at the boy. The boy yelled obscene words back at his parents.

The hogs became unsettled and began to tell the family to get out of the barn. Four Boy Two, Papa's prize Duroc boar (and that is his real name), though he was normally a very quiet and gentle hog, made deep throated noises in an attempt to frighten them off. But all he managed to do was add to the racket.

One of the boys picked up a clod of dirt in the hallway and threw it at the boar. About that time help arrived.

Steven, Mama and Papa's 13 year old grandson and his big black lab, Samson came running through the front door just in time to see the boy hit the boar, something that is not allowed, ever. The two of them herded the family out of the building in about 2 seconds.

Samson didn't make a sound. He showed those big white teeth and kept moving toward them. Steven didn't have to say a word until the family was back in their car. Then he spoke directly to the boys.

"Can't you read signs?" Steven looked squarely at the boy who threw the dirt clod. "We don't stand for anybody mistreating our hogs."

The boys had not taken their eyes off the dog. Neither had the parents.

In short order they were gone.

"Good dog," Steven praised Samson, giving him a hug and a pat on the head. Samson wiggled and whined happily as if to say, "You're welcome."

Steven had been away to Boy Scout Camp, but was glad to be back on the farm. He had missed his grandparents and the animals. But mostly, he had missed his dog.

That evening at the supper table Steven told his grandparents how he and Samson had scared off the abusive, uninvited, guests.

Papa laughed. "I couldn't have done it better myself, Steven. Thank you. You are a good Boy Scout and not too bad of a grandson."

"You're welcome, Grandpa. Now tell me about the Pot Bellies. How many do we have left?" the boy asked.

"We have 5 today. Tomorrow afternoon a fellow is bringing two more. I hope that's all for a while. Some times they come in faster than we can find good homes for them."

"There may be another pig going out," Mama said as she passed more hot rolls about. "Not a Pot Belly."

"Who are you talking about, Grandma?" Steven asked.

"I think Potsy wants to be adopted. I could be wrong. But you should have seen how happy she was when that little girl, Elsa, chose her over all the pet pigs. She loved it. I don't know if I could stand to part with her or not. She's so much like Priscilla and she's my pick of

Little Prissy's litter. Elsa's family is coming back tomorrow. They will try to decide between Lucky and Bonnie Lu. I'll pay close attention to Potsy's reaction with Elsa."

"Mama, I don't think they live in the country. What would they do with a farm hog like Potsy? I would hate to think what might happen to her when she got to big to be a house pet."

"She could end up as somebody's breakfast bacon!" Steven shook nervously at the thought of it.

"Oh my! I can't bear to think of that," Mama covered her eyes with her apron. "We do have a problem here, don't we? If she wants to go and we keep her, she'll hate us. And, if we let her go and they tire of her, we will hate ourselves."

"Don't worry about it honey," Papa said. "We'll never let her go into an uncertain situation like that."

Steven trusted his grandfather. The boy knew that once a pig was gone, his grandparents had little or no control over what became of it. Each time a pig left the farm, some risk was involved. One always hoped the pig would be treated fairly.

After supper Papa went back to the barn

to check on Starlight, one of the farm sows. Within a few hours, if all went well, she would have a new litter of pigs.

In the barn, Potsy was keeping a close eye on Arthur. When he stopped eating she nudged him back toward the feed.

"I just can't eat, Potsy. Sometimes I feel so cold and other times I feel hot and sick. I wish I could get to feeling better, but I'm not hungry. I try to eat so Mother won't worry about me. I even pretend to be eating. Food doesn't taste as good as it used to. None of it. I wish I could be more like you, Potsy. You *are* my favorite sister, and that's the truth."

Potsy rubbed her head up along the side of her brother's to give him a love. Sure enough, he was roasting hot.

Papa noticed that Potsy and Arthur were standing in a corner by themselves. Arthur looked terrible. The poor little fellow could hardly stand up. His legs were like rubber and his eyes were cloudy.

Papa telephoned down to the house to say he was leaving right away to take Arthur back to the doctor. He put a large towel in a box. Very gently he picked up the ailing pig and placed him on the towel. The pig was burning hot and too weak to resist being handled. Arthur didn't make a sound.

"Let's go see if we can get you some help, little fellow. Can't have you feeling so poorly."

Papa's many years of experience told him that Arthur's condition was critical. The pig was quiet for the three miles into Thomas Creek.

When they got to the Veterinary Clinic, Dr. Mike was working on a horse tied to the back of a pickup truck.

Papa waited for a few minutes until the vet was finished with the horse. Then he walked around to the passenger side of the car to fetch the little box and Arthur. Arthur was silent. He was perfectly still. The poor little pig had died on the way to town.

Papa was a tender-hearted man. Large tears rolled down his cheeks and splashed on his shirt. He would never get used to the death of one of his animals, no matter how many he lost.

Dr. Mike came over to Papa. When he saw that the pig was still, he understood Papa's tears.

Papa wrapped Arthur in the big towel and placed him back in the box.

He dreaded having to tell Mama and Steven.

Chapter 8.

A Messenger

That evening Arthur's lifeless little body was wrapped snugly and lovingly in a small quilt. Steven and his grandpa built a wooden box large enough to hold Arthur. He was taken to the Pet Cemetery back in the timbers and given a proper burial.

Arthur's life was short, but his family in the farrowing barn as well as the farm family would never forget him.

Sometime in the next few days, as was the custom, Mama would return to the cemetery with a smooth river rock large enough for Arthur's name and the years of his birth and death. In Arthur's case the birth and death year would be the same. The river rock would mark the spot where he was buried.

So many memories lingered in the Pet

Cemetery. As soon as the burial was completed, the somber family walked quietly to the house to retire for the evening.

Little Prissy was a wise old hog. When Papa failed to return with her baby, she knew the worst had happened. Prissy knew the symptoms all too well. She had lost a baby when she was younger to the same dread disease and had not forgotten.

Later on that evening, Mama paid a visit to Prissy's family.

"It was a combination of a virus and erysipelas, Prissy. You probably knew that already. His little body was just not stong enough to throw it off." Erysipelas is a common disease in young pigs. So much of the time it causes death.

Little Prissy looked away. She did not feel like talking.

For the next few days Prissy and her family were extremely restless and quiet. Someone might tell you that hogs don't mourn, that mothers don't miss their offspring when they die or are taken away. How do they know so much? It was obvious to the farm family that especially Prissy and Potsy were missing Arthur.

Elsa and her family came again to visit but once again left without a pig. Before they came, Papa turned Little Prissy and her family out to pasture, not wanting them available to Elsa's visits, not just yet.

After a few days Potsy was ready to turn her thoughts to Lucky and the life enjoyed by the Pot Bellies. Somehow, she didn't feel the same as before. Perhaps it was Arthur's death that brought about the change.

Potsy's mother had told her that she need not worry about Arthur. She said he would be well and happy in his new home with his hog ancestors, who had gone on before him. She felt sure he was with Priscilla. Prissy said Priscilla had told her about this place when she was a little pig. After hearing about it from Prissy, Potsy felt much better.

Steven showed up with Jocko, one of Tom Cat's sons. Potsy knew right away that this was a smart cat. Silly and somewhat conceited perhaps, but quite clever. She was eager to make friends with Jocko, and if he agreed, ask him to act as message carrier to Lucky. It was worth a try.

"I know what you're up to," Little Prissy said, smiling at her daughter. "I think you have made a wise choice, Potsy. This fellow Jocko, reminds me of his father. But, no cat will ever be as smart as Tom Cat." The sow was convinced of that.

"Potsy, if you want to get on Jocko's good side, pay him compliments. If he is truly T.C.'s son, he will love compliments," of that Little Prissy was certain.

Potsy stuck her nose through the boards in her fence as far as she could. She was looking at Jocko and trying to think of an appropriate compliment. After all, she was very young and it was her first try at this.

"Is your name really Jocko? It's such a beautiful name. Jocko." Potsy had gotten his attention. "My mother knew your father very well. Mother says he was the most handsome and smartest cat she had ever seen. I think you must look like your father." Now, Potsy had really gotten his attention.

Little Prissy was enjoying her daughter's cleverness. "Don't overdue it," she whispered to Potsy, who was doing an unbelievable job of conning the cat.

Jocko's face shaped a wide grin. So much so, he looked devilish in a cute sort of way.

Potsy had taken a giant step toward getting his attention and respect. For a moment, she was not sure how to proceed. Manipulating cats was new to her, but fun.

"You must be very clever having a father as smart as yours," she managed to say. "Your father delivered messages for my grandmother. She would tell him things and he would take her message to others ---"

Prissy got close and whispered into her daughter's ear. "Now say, 'but I suppose you wouldn't know how to do that'."

Potsy took her mother's advice.

"What makes you think that?" The cat flexed his muscles. With that, Jocko sprang to the top boards of the pen and jumped down into the pen with the family. What a surprise! How graceful he was.

"He is his father's son," Prissy said to herself.

Potsy stood and stared, tongue-tied and too embarrassed to speak. Her mother came to her rescue.

"I'm so glad you dropped in Jocko. It's been a long time since we've had anyone from your family visit us."

Jocko was feeling pretty special. Potsy figured he was an o.k. fellow. No doubt about it, she believed she had made a wise choice.

The whole idea behind having a messenger was to somehow convince Lucky to stay on the farm and refuse to be adopted. The pig didn't realize that Lucky didn't really have much to say about it. Papa and Mama were trying to find him a good home. One that was better than the one he came from.

More than anything, Potsy wanted Lucky to stay and be her friend. The question was, would the cat be able to convince the pig to at least try? We'll see.

Chapter 9.

The Message

During the next couple of days, Jocko was constantly in and out of Prissy's pen. You might call it "mutual attraction". In other words the cat had taken a liking to the family and the family to him.

What made Jocko so interesting to the pigs was the fact that he could come and go as he pleased. There was nothing on the farm he hadn't seen. He knew every inch of the house, the barns, sheds, the pasture and the woods.

For a cat who liked to hunt, there was no better place than the woods. But there was danger in the woods. Farm cats gone wild lived back there. Hiding in unsuspecting places, the wild cats loved to pounce on Jocko as he roamed the woods in search of a fat mouse.

Prissy's pigs were mesmerized by Jocko's

adventures. Spinning his tales with great style and showmanship, the cat claimed their attention. Each gory detail was exaggerated for effect. The "One Eyed Demon" was their favorite. In this story, Jocko lived through being chewed up and clawed to the point of death, by the meanest and most feared cat of all. It was the giant, killer cat, the one and only, One Eyed Demon.

No doubt about it, the cat was a great story teller. How much of it was true was a mystery to Prissy. She figured Jocko might be stretching things a bit just to entertain her babies. But it was all in fun and her babies did love it so.

"Why one night," he told them, "I was beat up and left for dead. I was stretched out stiff back by the creek for two days. Papa came by on his tractor and saw me lying there on the ground, bleeding. He picked me up and put me in the tool box. He and Mama took me right over there," he pointed to the office. "They worked on me for hours, patching me up." He stood up and flexed his muscles, again. "And it didn't hurt a bit." He added with a grin.

Like all the others, Potsy was glued to his stories. But enough was enough. The time had come to put her plan into action.

"Jocko, do you know the Pot Bellied pig named, Lucky?" she asked sweetly.

"I know everybody," the cat answered. "Lucky is the pig that ran away and hid from his owners in the Christmas tree farm. That pig won't be here long, he will find a good home. He's smart and he's got a great personality."

Potsy had no idea what a personality was, nor did she care. She was interested only in moving ahead with her plans.

"But that's the problem. I don't want Lucky to leave here. He was my very first friend. Please tell him for me, I want him to stay here. Tell him he must refuse to be adopted."

"But Potsy," the cat inquired, "What if he doesn't want to stay here? What if he really wants to go home with some nice family? How often can you make it down there to see him? How can you be friends?"

"I get to go down there when Papa cleans the pen," Potsy answered, trying to make a case.

Jocko looked around the pen. "This pen doesn't have to be cleaned every day. Why don't you find another friend? Besides, I think Lucky is already spoken for."

Now, Potsy was on the verge of tears. "No, that can't be true. Please talk to him right away, for me."

"Sure pig," the cat answered curtly. "But I don't think it will do a bit of good."

After having said that, the cat tried slithering through the 2x4's to make his exit. Finding his body a little too large, he jumped to the top boards and down onto the hallway floor. In a second he was out of sight.

The family, except Potsy, was sad to see him leave. The sooner he left, the sooner she would have an answer. Waiting would not be easy.

Papa and Steven sauntered in with a another new pig. The farm hogs overheard what they were saying about it.

"How do you know this is Lucky's brother, Grandpa?" Steven asked.

I know the lady who owned this litter," Papa answered. "This one is Oscar. A fellow bought it for his mother for her birthday. She was old, but she really wanted a pig for a pet. She had always wanted a pet pig. When she was a little girl on a farm in Iowa she fell in love with a little runt pig that she had raised on a bottle. Anyway, on Friday, she fell and broke her hip. Now she can't take care of him anymore. Her son asked me to find Oscar a good home. So, we'll try to find him a good home. Right, Steven?" Papa smiled.

"I guess so. Where do you find all of these people who want Pot Bellied pigs?" Steven asked.

"I don't, they find me. It's funny. The unwanted pigs find their way here and so do people who want them. The word has gotten around. People find us and your grandma and I are glad they do. We provide a service."

Lucky and Oscar were surprised and happy to see each other. Papa put Oscar in the pen next to Lucky. Cooper had gone to live with a family in Sweet Home. Papa said it was a match made in heaven. This family had a 12 year old boy, red haired and freckled face. When the family visited here, Cooper went to sleep in the boy's arms.

Potsy wondered if Oscar would be anything like Lucky. Maybe Jocko would give her a report on him too.

Potsy was not the only one who had taken a liking to Lucky. So had Steven. When Jocko came to visit, Steven was in Lucky's apartment, watching television. The boy knew that Jocko and Lucky were having a conversation, but he did not understand it. Steven wished for Mama. She'd know what they were saying.

Jocko did as Potsy asked. He tried to convince Lucky to stay on the farm.

"But cat, you understand. Tell that little

pig I have to go sometime, with somebody. We'd all like to stay. It's great here. But they can't keep us all. Besides, the Collins family is o.k. They want Bonnie Lu too. We know what the hold up is. Their daughter Elsa, wants Potsy and Potsy is not up for adoption. I have a feeling we will be leaving here with them soon."

Jocko listened. He understood what Lucky had to do. The Pot Belly was making a sensible decision. Explaining that to Potsy and helping her understand will not be easy. Lucky has but one choice available. If he doesn't go with this family, well, the next one might not be so nice. But on the other hand, if Elsa doesn't bond with Lucky soon, Papa won't let them have him. Everybody has to be satisfied before a pig leaves the farm. Or so Papa says.

If that is so, then how about Potsy? She will definitely not be satisfied if Lucky gets carried out the front door. And he probably will, real soon.

Chapter 10.

Two Pigs Are Adopted

Potsy drooped around for two days after Jocko reported back with Lucky's reply.

"He said he'd better take this good family while they're available," Jocko had told the unhappy pig. "He said good families are hard to come by."

It was Tuesday, the day for visitors. Late in the afternoon Elsa's family came again.

"Scrud!" Potsy said to herself. What a difference a few days can make. She still liked Elsa, but she wasn't ready to deal with her at the moment. For now at least, she hoped the little girl would stay away and mind her own business.

Chance followed Elsa's family into the barn.

"I suppose you want to go home with them too," Potsy complained to the cat. "You might as well, everybody else is."

"I don't know if I am up for adoption or not. I'm not a Pot Belly. Are you up for adoption?" Chance asked Potsy.

Before Potsy had an opportunity to answer, Little Prissy spun around and spoke angrily to the cat. "Well, she'd better not be. We aren't cut out for living in the house. We are farm hogs and proud of it. Our job has always been to raise healthy breeding stock for other farms. Our owner sees to it that we are sold to good farmers."

Prissy's pigs were curious and perhaps a little worried. After their mother's outburst they wanted to know more about what would become of them.

"It's nothing to worry about. When you are older you will understand your responsibility and duty in life more clearly. I want you to be proud of who you are. A few of us from a litter will always remain here, like I did. But don't worry about it, my children. You are much to young to be bothered about such things." Prissy hoped her pigs would take her advice.

Chance looked strangely at Prissy. He had heard a rumor and wondered why the news had not reached Little Prissy's ears. Chance was a nice cat and did not want to cause this family any undue worry. Afraid he might forget himself and tell the rumor, he hurried on down the hall.

Ordinarily, Papa kept a Pot Belly in the barn until the entire family bonded with it. It was Elsa's family. Tip and Alice Collins, their son Colin and daughter Angela, were getting on quite well with Bonnie Lu and Lucky. Elsa was the problem. She liked the two Pot Bellies and was nice to them and they to her, but she was not too excited about taking them home, like the others. Perhaps, Papa thought, in this case it might be all right. The family was good with the pigs. They lived in Thomas Creek, only 3 miles away. So, after considerable thought the family was given permission to take both Pot Bellies.

Seeing Lucky leave was unpleasant for Steven. He took off. The boy had grown fond of the pig but had said nothing to his grandparents about wanting to keep him.

Fortunately, Potsy and her family were unaware that the Collins family had come and gone with their new pets. Mr. Collins had parked his van by the back door. When they drove away, they were out of sight from Prissy's pen.

Before their departure, Elsa slipped away, ever so quietly, to say goodbye to the pig of her choice, Potsy. Finding them sleeping, she stood there for a few seconds and gazed lovingly.

She longed to hug Potsy's neck. A tiny tear fell from her eye as she whispered a silent farewell.

That evening Papa and Mama had unexpected visitors at the farmhouse, Mr. Collins and Elsa. Elsa's eyes were red from crying.

"What in the world is the matter?" Mama asked, putting her arms around the girl.

Elsa waited for her father to tell them.

"She won't stop crying. I had to promise I'd come and ask you folks if there is any way in the world she can have one of the farm hogs?"

Papa looked at Mama to see if she understood why they asked such a question.

"Elsa likes Potsy, and Potsy likes her," Mama told him.

To Mr. Collins she said, "Potsy is a farm hog. We have no intention of ever letting her leave the farm. Anyway, you folks live in town. You can get away with having a Pot Belly in Thomas Creek, but you would never be allowed to have a farm hog. Elsa is welcome to come here and visit whenever she likes. She can always be near Potsy and grow up with her."

Papa felt sorry for Elsa. "You have to understand something, Elsa. Potsy will not stay small. Within a year she will weigh well over 200 pounds. Oh, she'd be o.k. in the house for a while, but just a little while. Farm hogs grow fast. And then what would you do with her, send her to market? We could never let you do that. She belongs with Little Prissy." Papa made his case.

Elsa sniffled into a kleenex. "While Potsy is little I can keep her in the house. My Aunt Marj is on a farm. She said I could keep Potsy there. She has an empty barn and barn lot just sitting there. I can ride out to the farm on my bike and take care of Potsy. I just know Potsy would be happy. She will have the place all to herself."

Papa and Mama were both thinking about the same thing. Aunt Marj's place sounds like a lonesome place for a pig.

"Where is your Aunt Marj's place, Elsa?" Mama asked.

"About a mile from here on the way in to town. It used to be a goat dairy," Mr. Collins answered.

"I know the place," Papa replied. "It's where the family lived who used to own Piston, our burro. They moved away some years ago."

"Papa and I will have to talk this over. I know how much you like Potsy, Elsa. We have to be sure it's the right thing to do. We love Potsy too. All I can tell you this evening is, we will give it a lot of thought. We will let you know what we decide.

"Fair enough," Mr. Collins agreed.

Elsa did not like the idea of being put off. She wanted Potsy and she wanted her right now. But Potsy belonged to Papa and Mama. She was Little Prissy's and Little Prissy was Priscilla's. That's what makes her so special. And that's only part of it. Potsy had become very dear to Mama.

What will Potsy say?

Chapter 11.

Bad News

As you can well imagine, Elsa could not eat or sleep thinking about Potsy. Every time the phone rang, she raced to answer. Mama and Papa had no intention of making a quick decision. Something as important as this, will take time.

As for Bonnie Lu and Lucky, the first couple of days were fine. However, on the third day the two Collins kids got into a big fight over whose turn it was to feed the pigs. The argument did not get settled and the pigs did not get fed. And the arguments continued.

Lucky was mad. Bonnie Lu said it happened to her before. Her last owners were reported to the Humane Society for neglecting her. That's how Papa ended up with her. In fact that's how Papa ends up with a lot of pigs.

"This may be old business to you, Bonnie Lu, I've been hungry too. Really hungry. But I like to eat and I know where the food is. If I get hungry enough I will run off and go back to the farm. I know the way," Lucky said bravely.

"You can't do that. You might get run over by a car," Bonnie Lu replied.

"Don't worry about me. I won't go unless I have to," Lucky told her.

Back in the farrowing barn, Little Prissy's family watched Jocko jump the fence making his big entrance.

"Where have you been the last couple of days," Thomas asked. "We've missed you."

"I've been here and there. Several feline females enjoy my company," he grinned. "Visited with Piston, the burro, this morning. Went by to see Glory's new pigs. Caught a fat, yummy mouse in Johnson's hay field. What else do you want to know?"

"Yuck. How can you stand to eat a mouse. Doesn't it make you sick?" Potsy asked.

"You should try it sometime. Want me to bring you one?" Jocko smiled a silly smile, knowing full well pigs don't hunt or eat meat.

"No, never," Nel answered, making a face.

"We truly have different eating habits.

Cats even turn up their noses to fresh fruits and vegetables from the garden," Prissy told her babies. "Hard to believe."

"Have you seen Lucky?" Potsy asked eagerly, changing the subject.

Jocko looked surprised. The news of Lucky's departure had not reached their ears and the pig had been gone for a couple of days already.

The cat's good fortune was to roam around at his leisure and hear all the news, sometimes before it happened. Jocko did not want to be the one to tell Potsy.

Potsy repeated the question. "Well, have you seen Lucky today?"

Jocko shuffled his feed nervously. "Lucky?" he asked.

Potsy looked at the cat. Why was he hedging? The pig began to get suspicious.

"Is Lucky going out that front door today?" Potsy asked sadly.

Again, Jocko hesitated. Little Prissy watched as the cat postponed his answer. The little sow knew her daughter must be told the truth. She nodded her head at the cat, as if to say, "She has to know. Go ahead and tell her."

There was no getting out of it.

"No, Potsy," Jocko said, "Lucky is not

going out the front door today. He and Bonnie Lu went out the back door a couple of days ago with the Collins family. You've gotta understand pig, he really didn't have a choice. Remember what he said? He didn't want to go. All he could do was to take his chances with this family."

Potsy hung her little head, strolled over to the straw bedding, crumpled her small body down and sobbed bitterly. Seeing her cry was too much for Jocko. He wasted no time in getting out of the pen.

Sometimes when trouble and sorrow find you, they hang close by for a while and keep slapping you around. About an hour later, more bad new showed up. Jocko was back. Oddly enough, the cat believed his news was good enough to cheer Potsy up.

"Listen up, little pig," he said cheerfully. "I just heard something that will make you one happy pig. You aren't going to be separated from Lucky after all."

"What?" Potsy sprang to her feet grinning broadly.

"They might come back and get you too. Elsa, that girl, she wants you to come and live with her, or maybe live on her Aunt's farm, down the road," Jocko told her. "You'll be with Lucky after all."

Again, the thought that one of her children might be adopted out like a Pot Belly infuriated Prissy. The sow was so outraged her body shook as she turned to face the cat. Her eyes were filled with anger. The pigs ran to the far corner of the pen, for safety. She glared squarely at her daughter, as if to say, "What have you gotten yourself into?"

"But I --- I don't want to, ---I don't understand. Mother, can they do this to me," Potsy cried. "I do like Lucky and I do want him here, but I don't want to go away from the farm. What shall I do?"

Prissy took some deep breaths. Her anger softened. She looked at her sad little daughter. So young. So innocent. Not old enough to be aware of all the dangers in the life of a pig. Hogs have little control over their own destiny. But at least on this farm all the animals are treated well.

Is this what Potsy's curiosity, her desire for attention and perhaps her jealousy of the Pot Bellies had gotten her? How was the pig to know.

"Don't cry, Potsy. We will think of some way to get you out of this," her mother promised.

The cat felt pretty rotten, His news had not been good after all. He had misjudged the pig's intentions. Jocko had to admit, there was a lot he didn't know about pigs.

Perhaps he'd find a way to help her. Or was it too late all ready?

Chapter 12.

Running Away

No one was more surprised than Prissy when morning came and Potsy was not in the pen. She stood up with her front feet resting on the top 2x4's to have a look around and ask questions.

"Potsy is gone!" she exclaimed to all who could hear. "Has anyone seen her? Was there a stranger in the barn? Did that bothersome girl, Elsa, come and take her?"

Poor Prissy. She was frantic. None of her neighbors, including her older daughters, Penny and Patsy, in nearby pens had seen anything unusual.

Prissy was sure that this all had something to do with Potsy's interest in the Pot Bellies. Why hadn't she minded her own business? Had the worst happened already? Had she been plucked out of the pen in the night and carried away?

Prissy raised a ruckus to get Papa's attention as soon as he arrived that morning.

"What's the matter, girl? Why are you so upset?" Papa asked.

He checked her pen for snakes and rats, but saw none. All the while she was telling him, "Potsy is gone. Potsy has been taken away." But Papa did not understand. He only knew there was a serious problem. He called to Maggie who was just out the door, nosing around.

"Maggie, let's check out the barn for strangers. Prissy is trying to tell me something and I don't know what it is."

Papa and the dog gave the barn a good going over but saw nothing suspicious. While they were investigating, the rest of the hogs were raising a big fuss because Papa wasn't passing out the feed.

"I'll get to you in a minute," Papa yelled. He understood what they wanted well enough. He'd heard it for a good many years.

"I'd better phone down to the house and tell Mama," he told the dog, "she'll find out what's troubling our Little Prissy girl."

Mama lost no time in getting to the barn. Nor in getting to the problem.

In a matter of minutes, Mama knew the trouble. The first thing she noticed was that Potsy was missing. Prissy was telling her only that the pig was gone and she knew not where she'd gone or how she got out of the pen.

"Papa, come and look!" Mama shouted . "Potsy has been stolen out of the pen."

"What?" Papa hurried over to have a look. "You're right. Somebody had to take her. She's too little to jump out over the top by herself. Sorry girl, we'll find your baby," Papa said to the sow.

Papa checked to see if a lower board had come loose. Perhaps she had escaped that way. But the pen was intact.

"You never know about pigs. We've been surprised before when one climbed out. But this time I think you're right. Potsy is too little to crawl out." Mama promised Prissy that she and Papa would find Potsy if she was to be found.

Papa wasted no time. First he called the Collins family to see if they had taken Potsy. They had not. Papa advised Mrs. Collins that she not tell Elsa the bad news. Not just yet. After the call, Papa made a sign for the front yard. A lost pig sign. He offered a reward. "Potsy just couldn't disappear like that," he thought.

Oh no! Potsy had fooled everybody. She

had gotten out all by herself by climbing up the 2x4's and over the top. She had worked all night at getting out. She did not make it over the top the first time she tried, nor the second or third time. Each time she climbed up, she fell backwards. She'd lie there and take a little rest, and think what she had done wrong, and try again. She fell backwards so many times, her poor, tired, sleepy body ached all over. Trying to keep her escape a secret, she'd listen now and then to see if she had disturbed anyone.

Once she had made it to the top, she either jumped down or fell. She wasn't sure. It was a long distance for a little pig. Potsy landed on the ground in the hallway, on her hind feet, her front knees and her chin. She scooted for several feet before bumping her head on the metal grain barrel. But she never made a sound. Not one squeal. Not because she didn't want to. It hurt like the dickens.

Once she had gotten out, there was no turning back. She was determined to get out of the barn before Elsa showed up to take her away.

Bumping her head on that metal grain barrel, was something she hadn't counted on. The fall and the bump took her breath away. Her head still throbbed from the whack.

By the time her head cleared sufficiently, the sun was up and the birds were singing. If she wasn't quick about it, Papa would be in the barn and catch her. All her efforts would be in vain. So off she ran, as fast as her tired, stubby legs permitted, out the back door. Whether or not the hogs had seen her leave was of no consequence to her.

She had not given much thought as to where she would go. Once outside though, she spied the timber to the back of the farm.

The pasture behind the barn was all that stood between Potsy and the woods. She hoped for great hiding places in the trees and grass to nibble on. So anxious to get away, she failed to think of the dangers that might lie ahead. No one ever told her that the timber was unsafe for a young pig. Jocko had had trouble in the woods, but he was a cat.

Once in the pasture, the tall grass was great cover for her escape. She moved quickly. Just beyond the first few trees she came upon the Pet Cemetery where Arthur had recently been buried. Although she could not read the names on the river rocks, the bright little pig knew that the freshest dug grave belonged to her baby brother. She used the rock that marked his grave for a pillow and there she fell asleep.

A sudden noise awakened her when the sun was high in the sky. Potsy felt warm and comfortable, but hungry. When she opened her eyes she saw four friendly eyes looking back at her. No, it was not a squirrel wearing glasses. It was a doe and her young fawn.

"What are you doing here?" the fawn asked.

"I was running away from the barn and got sleepy," the pig answered.

"How could you run away from a barn? Was it chasing you?" the fawn asked innocently.

Potsy had to laugh. "No. I don't think the barn was chasing me."

The pig had an empty feeling in her belly. She had missed her morning pellets and her mother's milk. For the first time in her life, she was hungry.

"Where can I get something to eat?" she asked.

"There is plenty to eat if you know where to find it. Since you are new in the woods and are so young, I will tell you once. Afterwards you must look out for yourself," the doe told Potsy.

"O.K." Potsy didn't know what else to say, so she agreed.

The doe pointed to a path through the

woods. "Follow the path so you don't get lost. There is plenty of grass and berries everywhere. After a while you will come to the comfrey* patch. The leaves are delicious. Eat only what you need and take care not to damage the plants. Behind the comfrey patch runs a clear stream, fresh water for drinking and bathing. You will not be welcomed by everyone in the woods, so be very careful." After having said these things to the pig, the doe and her fawn ran off into the trees.

"Thank you," Potsy called after them. Although the pig had been away from her mother for a mere few hours, she missed her terribly.

She felt somewhat nervous about being alone in the woods. But she did as the mother deer had told her and headed down the path in search of food and water. All around her was tall green grass to nibble on. Soon she learned that her strong little nose came in quite handy for digging out tasty roots. While she enjoyed some earthly tidbits, an uncanny sensation came over her. The pig felt she was being watched. Looking carefully about, she heard nothing and she saw

----

*Comfrey - An herbal plant grown by Papa for livestock feed and medicinal purposes.

no one, but for some reason she knew something was watching her.

Ever so cautious, the pig continued on down the path, thinking that putting some distance between herself and *that* place, might be a good idea. Suddenly, she began to run as fast as she could, frightening unsuspecting animals along the way.

In her short life, she had seen only a few kinds of birds. An amazing variety lived in the timber. A splendid brown hawk flew from its nest. Then a beautiful red and yellow Western Tanager sang to her from high up in a dead fir tree.

Before long Potsy came out into an open field of plants having large green leaves, the comfrey patch. Soon after, she discovered how delicious the leaves were. When she had eaten enough to satisfy her hunger, taking care not to damage the plants as the doe had advised, she hurried on back to the stream and drank until her thirst was satisfied.

While Potsy was engaged in this refreshing moment, she caught a glimpse of her reflection in the water for the first time. At first she was startled and jumped back a bit.

"So that's what I look like," she said out loud. "Mama was right. I do look like Priscilla.

She turned her head from side to side, first smiling, then frowning. She tried wiggling her ears, crossing her eyes and, in general, had a good time.

Again, Potsy felt she was being watched. Who or what was keeping an eye on this little pig? Was it someone or some thing?

Chapter 13.

On Her Own

Steven and Samson paired up looking for Potsy. They searched all day without a clue. Mama was sure someone had stolen her. Papa was looking for strange car tracks. He had decided not to involve the sheriff just yet.

Little Prissy was sure no strangers were in the barn during the night.

"One of us would have seen or heard something and alerted the others," she told Mama.

Mama and Papa were totally baffled. "This is the strangest thing. Surely, the Collins family wouldn't take her without our approval," they agreed.

A search was made on the road in both directions, and the neighbor's fields and yards. Neighbors were called. But the calls produced nothing. No one had seen anything of a pig on the loose.

One of the neighbors, Carl Perry, also had a pet missing and that bit of news meant one thing, big trouble. The Perry's owned a bad tempered pit bull named Bic. He was kept on a long chain, outside. The chain had been attached to a post that had rotted away. The post split off in the night. Now, unfortunately, the dog had run away to God knows where.

Papa prayed he would not be the one to have to shoot that mean devil. Bic had already killed several of B.C. and Pam Nelson's sheep the last time he got out.

In the early afternoon, a few of the boys from Steven's Scout Troop came by to lend a hand, Tim McHenry and Ed Hudson, the Troop Leaders, and several boys including, Josh Percy, Mike Castle and Nick Barnett came to help. The Scouts were persistent. Every inch of the farm was covered again and again, but no one searched the timber.

The searching continued until it was too dark to see anything. Even then, a few boys carried on the search with flashlights, having one final look.

When the sun goes down, the woods get dark fast. Potsy was lonesome and confused.

How long could she survive in this strange new environment? She never stopped missing her mother, but going back to the barn was too risky. But after she had time to think about it, she wondered which could be worse, living here alone, or living with a family who did not take care of her. At least in the timber there was food and water, however, it was a lonely, scary place.

Luckily, Potsy stumbled on to the hollowed out base of a big Oregon pine tree. The mammoth old pine had grown peculiarly. The base had formed itself into a cave-like opening, a great shelter. The lower branches spread to about sixty feet in diameter, forming a giant umbrella.

Twice in the night she heard footsteps and a dragging noise outside the shelter. However, the pig remained quiet until whatever it was went away. The second time she was more startled than the first. She held her breath and waited. After it had gone she cried herself to sleep. After all, she was just a little pig.

Morning brought thick, miserable fog. A family of pushy, noisy squirrels wanted her out of the tree. They were climbing all over her and moving right in, swishing their big bushy tails around in the dry dust.

"Can't you wait just a minute until I get

out of here?" Potsy asked them. "I'm not so sure
this is your tree."

The squirrels only stared at Potsy and
made squirrel type noises. There wasn't one
friendly squirrel among them.

"You guys are just plain rude," the pig
announced as she vacated the nook in the tree
and headed out in search of some breakfast and
something to drink. Both were quite a ways
away. Hunting for food would take some getting
used to. In the barn, meals were brought in. No
one ever got hungry, ever. And, fresh water was
near all of the time.

****

Things were not going well for Bonnie Lu
and Lucky either. Mr. and Mrs. Collins trusted
two of their children, Colin and Angela, to take
care of their pets. But they weren't doing it. In
fact after a couple of days in the house, the kids
moved the pigs to an outside pen and away from
the supervision of their parents.

Elsa did not dislike the Pot Bellies, but she
did not claim them. As far as she was concerned,
they belonged to everyone else in the family. So,
Elsa felt no responsibility for the care and
feeding of Bonnie Lu and Lucky.

Lucky had made up his mind. He was
determined not to be starved out by another

neglectful kid. With this family it was two kids being neglectful.

Lucky was an independent little rascal and was already planning an escape. He knew good food and water awaited him in the farrowing barn. Lucky also knew that if Papa found out that he and Bonnie Lu were not being fed, he would have a fit.

In the mean time, back in the woods, Potsy was headed for trouble. All along she had thought something was watching her. Now she knew what it was. There on the path, blocking her way to the stream, stood the meanest looking dog she had ever seen. It was Bic, Carl Perry's pit bull. Potsy had no way of knowing that Bic was a vicious dog. The only dogs she'd known were Maggie and Samson and they were both good dogs. Having had no experience with one, how was she to know there was such a thing as a bad dog?

As Potsy trotted toward the dog, he began to show his teeth and growl. The pig stopped dead in her tracts. Now then, she began to fear the dog and with good reason.

Fortunately for Potsy, several full grown elk came loping through the trees, passing between herself and Bic. She spun around, changing directions and raced back to the tree where she had spent the night. Squirrels or not, she went flying inside to hide from the dog.

"Get out pig!" the eldest yelled.

"No! I won't and you can't make me!" Potsy yelled back. "There's a big mean dog out there. He won't let me by to the stream."

The squirrels demeanor changed at once. They too had seen the dog. Word had gotten to them already that Bic had killed and eaten several rabbits and a fawn. The fawn's mother fought courageously to protect her baby. Now she lay torn and bleeding from the pit bull's sharp teeth. If help does not arrive soon, she will surely die.

Bic's chain dragged through the fallen leaves making an eerie sound. The squirrels climbed the tree, leaving the pig with room enough in the back of the tree to be out of reach. The dog was too big for the small opening.

The pit bull approached the tree slobbering out of both sides of his mouth. He was looking for trouble.

The squirrels made a horrible racket. That aggravated the dog. He growled and snarled and pawed at the ground in front of the tree. He could taste that little pig. Thanks to the squirrels, the pig was safe for the moment. Nevertheless, Potsy's heart pounded like a big rock bumping down a flight of stairs. She wanted her mother.

After a few minutes that seemed like hours, the dog lost interest and trotted off.

The squirrels climbed down to survey the damage. The pig was still frightened but unscarred. Although the pig was grateful to the squirrels, she could not stand their chattering. After a while she announced to them that she was still very thirsty and must try to get to the stream.

"Getting a drink of water didn't used to be so dangerous," Potsy told them.

"Be careful. Watch out for that dog. He will kill again," the eldest squirrel warned.

"I'll listen for the chain," Potsy said. Cautiously, she strolled down the path. There was no sign of the dog. She ate green grass, comfrey leaves, drank her fill of water and even napped for a few minutes inside a hollow log, for protection from the dog or any other surprises these woods may hold in store for her.

Potsy began to root and nibble her way back to the squirrel's den. Suddenly, she heard a dull thud. Turning toward the sound she spied a deer who had fallen to the ground and was flailing to and fro as if in great pain.

Potsy felt it must be the doe who had been

attacked by the pit bull. The poor thing was covered with fresh blood from several bites and gashes in her body. It was the same doe who had given her directions. The pig was sorry to learn that it was her fawn who had been killed.

"Oh, if I were as big and tough as Four Boy Two, Papa's prize boar, I'd whip that dog," Potsy thought.

Potsy knew she must go for help, even if it meant having to go back to the barn. She must tell her mother so her mother could get help.

Nothing else mattered now. The kind, caring little pig put the doe's life ahead of her own problems.

She must get help as quickly as she could.

Chapter 14.

More Trouble

Potsy ran, heading toward the pasture and the barn. When the Pet Cemetery came into view she knew she was going in the right direction. Suddenly, she heard the sound of that cussed chain and she knew the chain was attached to a killer dog. Bic's loud barks and bellows peeled the morning air. The sounds were terrifying to the pig as she raced frantically through the cemetery, darting to the left and the right, hoping to get help for the doe.

In one broad lunge, Bic, barking savagely, slapped at Potsy, rolling her across the ground.

The loud barking did not go unheard. Samson heard it and so did Maggie. So did Lucky, who had run away again, and was heading down the highway roadside ditch toward the farm.

Potsy got up, shook herself, and gave Bic a good telling off.

"What is the matter with you, dog? Why are you being mean to me? You hurt me! Don't do it anymore!"

Again Bic pounced on the pig landing squarely on top of her back. Potsy managed to wiggle out. The dog whipped his head toward the pig's and bit her hard on the right ear, slicing the hide in two equal parts. The ear drooped. It was a bloody mess.

Potsy got away and ran behind a large, Oregon pine. The pig had an idea. The dog began to chase her around and around the tree. Each time around, the dog's chain wrapped tighter around the tree's wide trunk. Even though Potsy's ear hurt like the dickens, she was beginning to enjoy outsmarting the dog. One more time around the tree and the dog was so wound up he flopped helplessly down on his side.

"There, you dumb dog! Let me see you figure that out." The pig laughed at the dog lying there with a stupid look on its face. He didn't have sense enough to unwind himself. Potsy was glad about that.

Samson and Maggie showed up out of nowhere, barking their heads off.

"Where were you when I needed you?"

Potsy asked.

Maggie saw the pig's bloody ear and began to whine. Samson stood there and barked at Bic. Bic barked back at Samson. The noise was hurting Potsy's wounded ear.

Suddenly, Steven came running toward them, followed by Mama and Papa. They'd all heard the ruckus and came to investigate.

"Potsy, is that you?" Steven shouted, giving the pig a big hug.

"What is going on here?" Papa asked. "It looks like that stupid pit bull has been at Potsy's ear."

Then from back in the woods came this mournful sound of pain. Potsy ran back down the path toward the sound.

Just as she hoped they would, the family heard the cries and followed along behind.

Potsy knew it was the deer. The doe had not moved. Potsy stopped and stood by the poor suffering animal.

"Oh my, Potsy, what has happened here?" Mama said sadly.

"Some more of that dog's handywork, no doubt," Papa noted. "The poor thing has lost a lot of blood, but it's clotting. She'll be weak for a while but I believe she'll make it. I'll keep an eye on her so she gets grass and water."

Potsy

Potsy knew Papa would take care of her.

"What are you going to do about the pit bull?" Mama asked.

"I'll go call Carl and tell him that his ridiculous dog is in my timber and he's tied himself to a tree," Papa laughed.

"Be sure to tell him what he did to our pig and the doe," Mama added.

Potsy wished she could tell them about the fawn and the rabbits.

Steven had his hands full. Samson kept barking and wanting to chastise Bic.

"Just leave that mutt right where he is, Samson," Steven told his dog. "I hope he gets what's coming to him."

Potsy's ear was really hurting her. Even though the blood had stopped spurting out, mending the long gash required Papa's expert knowhow. Right now it was split clean down the middle. Pig ears come up to a peak. Potsy had two halves coming up to a peak and both were drooping.

Potsy had decided to go along peaceably with the others. The fight was gone out of her. "After all," she told herself, "I am only a farm hog, nobody special, and who cares what happens to me anyway." Little Prissy would be furious with her daughter if she heard her say that.

The fog lifted and the sun came out to brighten up an eventful morning. All of them, Papa, Mama, Steven, Potsy, Samson and Maggie walked back through the pasture toward the barn.

Papa kept saying he'd like to shoot that pit bull. Steven always agrees with his grandpa, because grandpa is usually right.

It was a day for surprises. When they went in the back door of the barn, there was Lucky, running up and down the hallway. He was trying to get into his old pen.

Mama started laughing really hard. "These pigs! Will they ever stop surprising us with the unexpected? What is Lucky doing back and how did she get here? And, will somebody tell me how Potsy got out and what was she doing in the timber? What will happen next? This is supposed to be a peaceful, country, farm home. Well, I suppose I had better go call the Collins family and ask them a few quesions."

"And the first one should be, why was Lucky allowed to get out on the highway? They'd better have some good answers or no pigs of ours will ever go to that place again."

Potsy heard what Papa said and understood. If that was true, maybe she wouldn't be sent there after all.

Steven started to put Potsy back in her pen.

"Take her on up to the office, Steven, I have to fix her ear," Papa said.

"Do we have to call the vet?" Steven asked.

"No, I can handle this one myself," he answered.

In no time at all Potsy's ear was treated and taped. Papa had sprayed some blue stuff on it to stop the hurting. The pig was given a hug and a handful of grapes for being such a good patient.

Potsy was one happy pig to be back home with her family. Prissy asked lots of questions, one after the other, but the little pig did not hear. She was sound asleep on the fresh wheat bedding.

Lucky ate as if he was starved to death. Papa didn't like that at all.

"Didn't they feed you, Lucky?" he asked, as he watched the pig eat and drink. "I think I'll make an unexpected visit over there and see about Bonnie Lu. She may be back here too before the day is over."

By evening chore time there was a lot to talk about. Steven's friends returned to search some more for Potsy. Josh came, and Mike and Nick. Since the search was over, the boys decided to celebrate by having a cookout in the back yard.

Mama left the boys in charge of the cooking. After all, they were all experienced campers and good cooks. They did not need her.

She still had questions about Potsy and wanted answers. So, with nothing else to do at the moment she headed for the barn.

She lost no time in getting to Little Prissy's pen and making herself at home. She learned how Potsy had somehow managed to climb up the 2x4's and jump over the top. Remarkable! She heard about the death of the fawn and the courageous mother who fought the attacker.

Potsy waited for Mama to say that she would not be adopted by Elsa, but Mama did not say it. Feeling sad and tired, the poor little pig put her head on her mother's leg and fell asleep.

Chapter 15.

A Misunderstanding

The family sat in the back yard and ate hamburgers, corn on the cob and drank ice cold lemonade.

Steven was anxious to know more about the fate of the pit bull. "Tell us what Mr. Perry is going to do about his dog," he begged.

"Carl is a good man and a good neighbor," Papa explained. He didn't want Steven thinking anything bad about the fellow. "He just happens to own a bad dog. Carl can't figure out how his dog got so mean. He said he and his wife would talk to the sheriff and try to figure out what to do with the dog. But one thing I know, that dog will never bother anybody again. This is twice he's gotten out and killed and injured animals. He's not likely to be given a third chance."

"Is he still tied to the tree," Josh asked.

"No, I saw Carl and his wife coming out of the timber with him," Papa answered.

"Now would anybody like to know how Lucky got away from the Collins family?" Mama asked, with a big grin on her face. It was obvious she was glad the pig was back. Everyone wanted to know about Lucky.

"Well, the pigs got hungry. The kids were fighting over who was going to feed them, so the pigs didn't eat," Mama explained.

"I thought it might be something like that," Papa said gravely.

"It wasn't Elsa," Mama continued. "At first she wanted Potsy for a pet."

"You guys weren't really going to let her have Potsy, were you?" Steven asked.

"No, it was just a momentary consideration because the little girl fell in love with that pig. You know how it is when you take a special liking to an animal. We've all done it," Papa answered.

"At first Elsa wanted Potsy for a pet, real bad," Mama said. "She really loves her. But, when she found out how her brother and sister had treated Bonnie Lu and Lucky, she felt sorry for Bonnie Lu and took an immediate liking to her. Lucky had already hit the road when the family found out what the kids were doing, or not doing, I should say. Now, Elsa has taken Bonnie Lu over. Elsa has a kind heart."

"Elsa told her brother and sister they better never come near *her* pig," Papa laughed. "I'll keep and eye on the family for a while. I'll make neighborly visits. When I left from over there, Elsa was loving that pig to death and getting ready to give her a bath. Bonnie Lu will be alright. She seems to like Elsa."

"What about Lucky, Grandpa?" Steven asked.

"I agreed with Mr. Collins. Maybe one pig is enough for them for now. Anyway, I don't think Lucky cares to go back to them. Lucky kept on rooting until he had a hole made under the fence just big enough to get his body through. Then down the roadside ditch he ran, all the way home. Micky Clack said when she saw that pig running down the ditch, she knew it had to be one of ours, heading home. So she didn't even bother with it."

"Grandpa, can we keep Lucky? I've kinda gotten attached to him myself." Steven asked.

"Well of course you can keep him, Steven. I had no idea you wanted him or I wouldn't have given him away in the first place," Papa said.

"Now you have a dog and a pig," Mama

smiled at her grandson.

"I think I'll teach him to jump on the trampoline with me," Steven told his friends, who all thought that was a nutty idea.

"There is one remaining question. Why did Potsy run away? What happened? Why did she want to get away from her family?" Mama wondered.

"Well, why don't you ask that little sow in the barn that you talk to all the time," Papa teased. He loved tormenting Mama about talking to the hogs.

"All right, I will," she smiled and off to the barn she went.

Steven's friends were leaving for home. He thought now would be a good time to go to the barn and let Lucky know that this would be his home forever. Lucky loved the news. He could hardly believe his good fortune. And being Steven's pet was a big plus.

"Why don't we let you out of there so we can run around for a while?" Steven said to the happy pig.

Down at Little Prissy's pen, Mama was leaning over the boards to have a chat. When Steven came by with Lucky, she was surprised that Potsy did not seem at all interested in the pig.

"What's the matter Potsy? Don't you like Lucky anymore?" Mama asked.

She did not answer, but her mother did some explaining.

"Potsy thinks associating with the Pot Bellies and Elsa Collins is what got her into trouble in the first place."

"Trouble?" Mama asked. "What trouble?"

"Oh she got herself into trouble all right. My little daughter got to feeling sorry for herself because the Pot Bellies got all the attention," Prissy told Mama.

Mama was taken by surprise. "But that isn't true. Everybody is treated equally here."

"What Potsy meant was attention from the visitors who come to see the Pot Bellies," Potsy explained. "When she noticed that the Pot Bellies have carpets, televisions and furniture like the farmhouse, she got the idea that we are somehow inferior to those pigs," That idea was offensive to Little Prissy. She was a farm hog and proud of it.

Mama looked at Potsy who sat on her hindside looking up and listening to every word.

"Potsy, honey, you are not inferior to anybody. Why, Papa's farm friends are always trying to get him to enter you guys in the County and State Fairs. They say that your family would win all the ribbons. No Potsy, you are not inferior to anyone. In fact you are better than the finest hogs found anywhere. You are the best."

Mama's defense of Prissy's family pleased Potsy a lot. She stood and flexed her muscles a little, like she'd seen Jocko do. Her mother nodded as if to say, "See there. I told you so."

Mama tried to explain to the confused little pig and hoped she would understand.

"The Pot Bellies are being trained to live in a house. They will be somebody's pet. Papa and I have provided household settings for those pigs only because its necessary. When the time comes for them to be adopted, living around furniture will be familiar to them and they will quickly adjust in their new home. Don't you see?" Mama hoped she did.

"Potsy liked the attention Elsa gave to our family," Prissy told Mama. "But when that sweet little girl insisted on taking my baby home for a pet, that's when Potsy became scared and confused."

"Then it's all a big misunderstanding. Potsy heard that Elsa wanted her." Mama felt bad about all of it. "Just when Papa and I think we know everything there is to know about hogs, we learn something new."

"I tried to warn Potsy, poor thing. I told her I would never get to see her again if she got carried out under somebody's arm." Prissy remembered.

"Not even all the Pot Bellies want to be adopted. Look at Lucky. He got out, walked right up the roadside ditch and headed home," Mama laughed. "Papa and I were sad when we thought you wanted to leave us, Potsy. But we wanted you to be happy and were just about ready to let you go if you wanted to. Poor Potsy. I am so sorry girl." Mama went inside the pen, sat down by Potsy and spoke to her. "It's all a big mistake, Potsy. Papa and Steven and I want you right here with us. Elsa can come and visit you any time she wants to, but you are staying here. Lucky is staying too. Now that he is Steven's pet, you'll see him a lot. In another week, you'll be in the pasture with him for a little while, everyday."

Potsy wanted to make sure she heard it from Mama before she allowed herself to get too excited. When she realized she was home for good, her happy smile returned. And knowing that she and Lucky could be friends, was wonderful.

So everything worked out all right after all. Steven came by with Lucky. He opened the gate and invited Potsy to come for a romp with them. Perhaps he'll put both pigs on the trampoline. Wouldn't that be a sight to see?

The End

To order books by this author.   August 1997
If these books are not available from your local bookstore, you may purchase directly from the publisher. Mail your order with your check or purchase order to: Jordan Valley Heritage House, 43592 Hwy. 226, Stayton, Or. 97383.

Books by Colene Copeland:

Priscilla (hc)	$9.95
Priscilla (pb)	$4.95
Little Prissy and T.C. (hc)	$9.95
Little Prissy and T.C. (pb)	$4.95
Piston and the Porkers (hc)	$9.95
Piston and the Porkers (pb)	$4.95
Mystery in the Farrowing Barn (hc)	$9.95
Mystery in the Farrowing Barn (pb)	$4.95
Wanted: Pot Bellied Pigs (hc)	$9.95
Wanted: Pot Bellied Pigs (pb)	$4.95
Potsy and Lucky (pb)	$4.95
*All six of the above paper back books	$25.00
Magic Cellar (hc)	$8.95

Book by Christina McDade:

Apples in the Sky (pb)	$3.95

Postage and handling for 1 book $1.25, 2 books $2.00. For each additional book add .50 cents.

Thank you.   503-859-3144